MIDNIGHT LIBRARY

Copyright © 2014 by Kazuno Kohara
Published by Roaring Brook Press
Roaring Brook Press is a division of
Holtzbrinck Publishing Holdings
Limited Partnership
175 Fifth Avenue,
New York, New York 10010
mackids.com
Published in Great Britain by
Macmillan Children's Books, London
All rights reserved

Library of Congress
Control Number: 2013943785

Roaring Brook Press books may be
purchased for business or promotional
use. for information on bulk purchases please
contact Macmillan Corporate and Premium Sales
Department at (800) 221-7945 x5442 or by email
at specialmarkets@macmillan.com.

First American edition 2014
Printed in China by Wing King Tong Paper Products Co. Ltd.,
Shenzhen, Guangdong Province

3 5 7 9 10 8 6 4 2

to my grandparents

ROARING BROOK PRESS
NEW YORK

THE MIDNIGHT LIBRARY

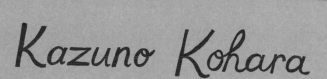

Kazuno Kohara

Once there was a library
that opened only at night.

A little librarian worked there
with her three assistant owls.

Every night, animals came to the library from all over the town.

And the little librarian and her three assistant owls helped each and every one find a perfect book.

The library was always busy, but it was also a
peaceful and quiet place. Until one night when . . .

A band of squirrels began to play music!
"Shhh!" said the little librarian.
"Please be quiet in the reading room!"

"We're sorry," said the squirrels. "But we're trying to find a good song for our next concert."

"Then follow me!" said the little librarian.

And she showed the squirrels to the activity room.

Silence settled upon the library once more, while the band played their instruments as loud as they liked.

Later that night, the little librarian
was busy putting books away,
when suddenly it started to rain!

"Oh dear!" said the little librarian.
"There must be a hole in the roof!"
But sitting on top of a bookshelf she found . . .

A wolf! And she was crying
so much her tears fell like rain.

"What is the matter, Miss Wolf?"
asked the little librarian.

"Something very sad happened in my story and I can't read it any more," replied the wolf.

"Please don't cry," said the little librarian. And she took Miss Wolf to the storytelling corner.

They read the book
together until gradually
the wolf began to smile.

The librarian and her assistants
knew the story had a very happy ending.

DING! DING! The bell rang out as the sun came up. It was time for everyone to go home.

One by one, the animals left the Midnight Library.

All except one new visitor . . .

A tortoise, reading slowly in a corner.
And he would NOT move!

"I must stay until I finish reading this book,"
said the tortoise. "I only have 500 pages left!"

"Let us make you a library card," said the little librarian.

"Then you can borrow this book and take it home with you!"

"How wonderful," said the tortoise. "And how lucky I am!"

"Goodbye, Mr. Tortoise, have a good day!"

The three owls and the little librarian gave
the empty library a good dust and a sweep.

Then finally it was time to find one last book.

A very special book . . .

A book of bedtime
stories for three
sleepy owls.

Sleep
tight!